Put Beginning Readers on the Right Track with
ALL ABOARD READING™

The All Aboard Reading series is especially for beginning readers. Written by noted authors and illustrated in full color, these are books that children really and truly *want* to read—books to excite their imagination, tickle their funny bone, expand their interests, and support their feelings. With four different reading levels, All Aboard Reading lets you choose which books are most appropriate for your children and their growing abilities.

Picture Readers—for Ages 3 to 6
Picture Readers have super-simple texts, with many nouns appearing as rebus pictures. At the end of each book are 24 flash cards—on one side is the rebus picture; on the other side is the written-out word.

Level 1—for Preschool through First-Grade Children
Level 1 books have very few lines per page, very large type, easy words, lots of repetition, and pictures with visual "cues" to help children figure out the words on the page.

Level 2—for First-Grade to Third-Grade Children
Level 2 books are printed in slightly smaller type than Level 1 books. The stories are more complex, but there is still lots of repetition in the text, and many pictures. The sentences are quite simple and are broken up into short lines to make reading easier.

Level 3—for Second-Grade through Third-Grade Children
Level 3 books have considerably longer texts, harder words, and more complicated sentences.

All Aboard for happy reading!

To my stellar brother, John Brennan—P.D.

For the Kettners, past & present—S.M.

Special thanks to Dr. Michael Allison, NASA, the Goddard Institute for Space Studies.

Photo credits: front and back cover, NASA/JPL/Caltech; p. 13, US Geological Survey/SPL/Photo Researchers, Inc.; pp. 16-17, NASA/JPL/Caltech; p. 19, NASA/JPL; p. 27, NASA/SPL/Photo Researchers, Inc.

Library of Congress Cataloging-in-Publication Data

Demuth, Patricia.
    Mars : the red planet / by Patricia Demuth ; illustrated by Stephen Marchesi with photographs.
        p.   cm. — (All aboard reading)
    Summary: Reviews the history of Earth's observation of the red planet since ancient times, explores the results of modern scientific studies carried out by telescope, satellite, and landing probe, and speculates on a future human landing
    1. Mars (Planet)—Juvenile literature. [1. Mars (Planet)] I. Marchesi, Stephen, ill. II. Title. III. Series.
QB641.D46   1998
523.43—dc21   98-13996
                                                                                                          CIP
ISBN 0-448-41888-6 (GB)   A B C D E F G H I J   AC
ISBN 0-448-41843-6 (pbk)   A B C D E F G H I J

ALL
ABOARD
READING™
Level 3
Grades 2-3

MARS
The Red Planet

By Patricia Demuth
Illustrated by Stephen Marchesi

With photographs

Grosset & Dunlap • New York

On a clear night you can look up and
scc a glowing red dot in the sky. It is not
a star. It is a planet. A red planet.

Long ago the ancient Romans gave
this planet its name. Red was the color
of blood. Red was the color of war. So the
Romans called the planet Mars, after their
god of war.

Mars is one of nine planets that circle the sun. It is Earth's neighbor. Mars is only about half the size of Earth. And it is much colder on Mars than it is on Earth.

Sun

Mercury

Venus

Earth

Mars

Jupiter

Saturn

Still Mars is the planet most like Earth. Its days last about twenty-four hours. It also has an atmosphere—a layer of gases around it. And most important of all, Mars has water. The north pole and the south pole of Mars are covered with icecaps.

Pluto

Uranus

Neptune

Because Earth and Mars are alike, scientists have long wondered: Since there is life on Earth, could there also be life on Mars?

In 1877, some people thought there was proof. An Italian astronomer was studying Mars through his telescope. He saw a series of straight lines on Mars. He called these lines "canali." In Italian that means "channels." But when the word was put into English, it became "canals." It was one little word. But it was a big mistake.

Channels are natural waterways. But canals must be built. So the idea spread that the "canals" on Mars had been built by Martians. Smart Martians.

Before long, there were lots of wild stories about creatures on Mars. In some stories, Martians were little green men who rode in flying saucers. In other stories, Martians were scary and evil. Some of these stories made people afraid of the red planet. What happened in 1938 is proof of that.

On October 30, 1938, an actor named Orson Welles read a story on the radio. The story was called "War of the Worlds." It was about Martians attacking the earth. Welles read the story as if it were a newscast. There were "eyewitness" reports. They said that Martians had already burned the state of New Jersey. They were marching on New York. They were tearing up railroads. They were spreading poison gas.

Many people thought the story was real. Panic spread across America. People fled their homes. They thought it was the end of the earth.

Of course, scientists knew that wild stories about Martians were untrue. But the question still remained: Could anything live on Mars?

Since 1600, scientists with telescopes had been able to study Mars. If they were going to learn more, they needed a much closer look.

In 1964, the American space agency, NASA, sent a spacecraft to Mars. It was called the Mariner 4. It did not carry any people on board. But it did carry special cameras.

The Mariner 4 flew more than 300 million miles. That was much farther than any spacecraft had ever gone before. As the Mariner flew by Mars, it took the first close-up pictures.

The pictures were disappointing to people who had hoped to see signs of life. Nothing grew on Mars, nothing at all. Mars looked like the moon—a dead world. Its surface was spotted with craters. They were formed by space rocks that had crashed into Mars billions of years ago.

In 1971, another spacecraft reached Mars. This time the spacecraft went all the way around the red planet. As it made its orbit, it took many pictures of different parts of Mars. The photos from this trip showed a much more interesting world.

Scientists saw that Mars has huge volcanoes. In fact, it has the largest volcano on any planet. The volcano is named Mount Olympus, and it towers fifteen miles high!

Mars has giant canyons, too. The biggest is called Mariner Valley. It would stretch all the way across the United States. We think the Grand Canyon is big. But Mariner Valley is ten times longer, twenty times wider, and twice as deep. What made such a big crack on Mars? An ancient earthquake—or, rather, Marsquake!

The 1971 orbiter made another big discovery. Water once flowed on Mars. Now the planet is bone dry. There is no running water on it. But the photos from 1971 showed ridges on the surface of Mars. Scientists could tell that these ridges had been made by water. Running water, not ice. So long ago, Mars must have been much warmer. Maybe, just maybe, tiny forms of life had lived on Mars during that warmer, wetter time.

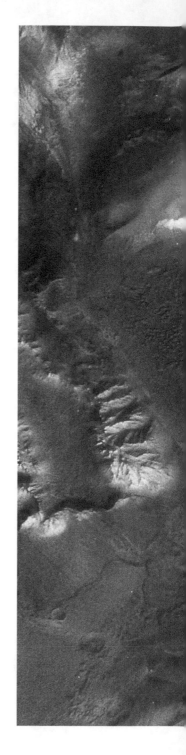

17

So far, the trips to Mars had been fly-bys. The next step was to land a spacecraft right on the planet. That happened in 1976. Two landers touched down on Mars within six weeks of each other. The close-up photos they took were amazing. The ground appeared orange-red, like rust. Even the sky was red—the same color that the Romans had noted thousands of years before.

Twenty years went by without another
successful landing on Mars. Then, in
December 1996, the Pathfinder was
launched. On board was a rover—a special
little car made to run on Mars. It was the
first vehicle ever made to get around on
another planet.

For seven months the Pathfinder traveled at the screaming speed of 60,000 miles per hour. By July 1997, it was very close to the red planet.

Right before landing, a giant parachute opened to slow down the spacecraft. Air bags puffed out on all sides and small rockets fired. When the Pathfinder landed on Mars, it was going just twenty miles per hour. It bounced like a beach ball on the air bags. Then it rolled to a rest.

It was a perfect landing!

Back on Earth, cheers broke out at NASA headquarters for the Pathfinder space mission. It was July 4th—a great day to celebrate.

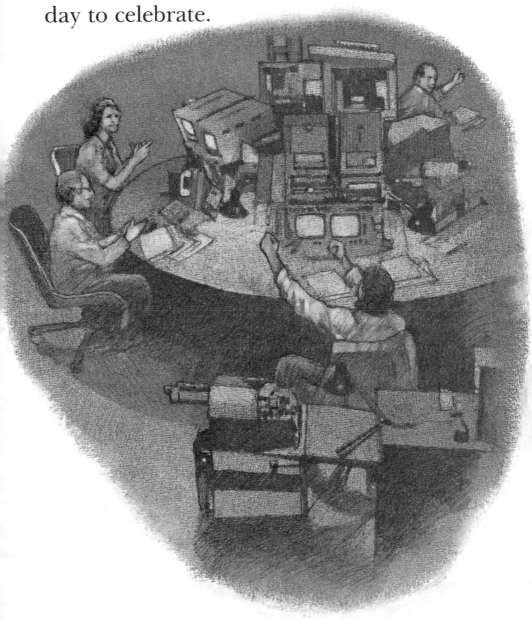

Then, on a computer screen, the scientists watched what happened next on Mars. The Pathfinder opened. The little rover inside rolled away onto the surface of the planet.

The rover had six wheels. It was only about the size of a microwave oven—one foot tall, two feet long. It had a computer for a brain. It was powered by the sun.

For a back-up, the rover carried D-cell batteries. They were very much like the kind you would use in a flashlight.

The rover's name was Sojourner—after Sojourner Truth. She was a former slave who fought to free other slaves. A twelve-year-old girl from Connecticut suggested the name. Sojourner Truth was her hero. Scientists also liked the name because Sojourner means "traveler."

Ready to work, the rover nosed up to a big rock. It looked like a sleeping bear, so NASA scientists called it Yogi. The rover zapped Yogi to take an X-ray. Now scientists could tell what the rock was made of. Then the rover rambled over to the next rock.

NASA controlled the rover from Earth. It was a little like running a remote control toy car. But there was a big time difference. It took eleven minutes for signals to travel from Earth to Mars. The rover moved very slowly—just two feet per minute. That way scientists had better control of where it was going.

Unlike the busy little rover, the Pathfinder stayed put. It took pictures, too, and beamed them back to Earth.

The Pathfinder took this picture of the
landing spot. It is as dry as a desert there.
Unlike a desert, though, it is always very
cold. By day, it may be 10 degrees
Fahrenheit. By night, it falls to minus 125
degrees Fahrenheit!

The scientists at NASA were not the only ones who got to see the Pathfinder's pictures right away. People all over the world could see them on their computers. Through the Internet, people saw pictures taken on Mars just a few hours earlier.

For three months, the Pathfinder took photos and Sojourner traveled about the red planet. The mission was a big success. There are plans for ten more spacecraft to go to the red planet.

In 2005, the U.S. space agency NASA hopes to be able to send a spacecraft to Mars and back. It will be the first round trip to Mars. On board will be a robot. It will collect rocks and soil and return the samples to Earth.

A great dream lies ahead for the year 2020. By then, scientists want to land human explorers on Mars. It will be a long and hard trip. It takes two days to get to the moon. But it took the Pathfinder seven months to reach Mars. And there was no way to get it back home. Scientists are working out ways to make the long round trip to Mars safe for humans.

Perhaps someday people will build cities on Mars. Then perhaps people on the red planet will gaze up into the night sky and look for a beautiful blue dot. Earth.